P9-CEH-298

LONG SHOT FOR PAUL

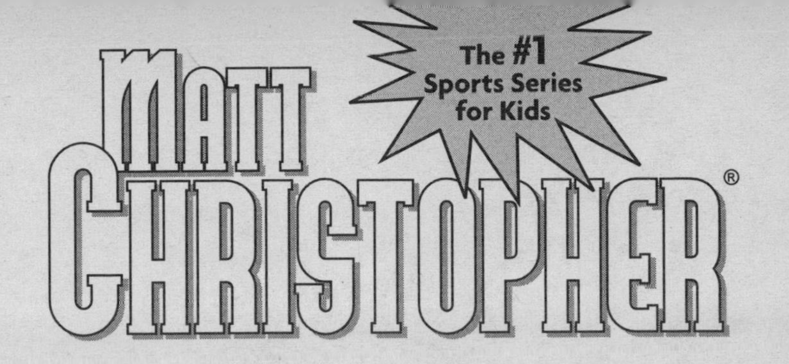

LONG SHOT FOR PAUL

LITTLE, BROWN AND COMPANY
New York A Time Warner Company

ISBN 0-316-14244-1 (pb)

Library of Congress Control Number 66-14906

20 19 18 17 16 15

COM-MO

Printed in the United States of America

To John, Ann Marie, Tina Rose,
Christopher and Russell

LONG SHOT FOR PAUL

They were in the driveway — Glenn, Judy, and Paul — throwing the basketball to each other.

Glenn saw that Paul caught the passes fairly well, but that he missed the hard ones. He would have to improve on his catching. The guys on the Sabers team threw the ball really hard at times. You had to in a game. And, if Paul didn't learn to catch hard passes, as well as throw them, he might *never* be able to play with the Sabers.

Just then Paul caught a pass that Judy had thrown far to his left. It seemed to surprise even Paul. His eyes popped wide, his mouth dropped open, and he laughed.

"What do you think of *that* catch?" he cried.

"Nice, Paul!" Glenn shouted, breaking into a laugh too. "Just keep your eyes on the ball!"

Paul played volleyball at Moreland, the school for special needs children that he attended. That was why he was able to catch a ball fairly well. But Moreland did not have a basketball court. Paul had never played basketball, except here at home where he played most often by himself and with Glenn. Dad had built the backboard onto the garage only last week. It was then that Glenn had decided to teach Paul to really play the game. It would help Paul a lot to make friends, something he had too few of.

Paul played mostly by himself, except when Glenn and Judy played with him. He even played with Judy's dolls sometimes.

"You don't want to be a sissy, do you?" Glenn had once asked him. "Dolls are for girls, not guys."

Paul had looked at him with hurt in his eyes, and Glenn was sorry he'd said anything. He realized it would be wrong to make Paul give up something he enjoyed.

They had learned Paul was developmentally disabled a long time ago, when Mom had taken Paul to a doctor to find out why he was so slow in learning anything. The news had struck Mom and Dad hard. Mom didn't want to believe it for a while. She thought the doctor was wrong. So they had another doctor examine Paul and this doctor said the same thing that the first one did.

After that things had become different

around the place. For example, Judy used to yell at Paul for something he had done and he'd get so mad he'd run to her room, pick up her reading book, and tear out some of its pages. Glenn used to yell at him for doing things now and then too, such as taking that special model destroyer of Glenn's without asking for it. Paul took this model, which was never meant to touch water, and set it afloat in the tub.

Another time Paul had scrawled with colored crayon on the pages of one of Glenn's schoolbooks. Asked why he had done it, he just shrugged. So Glenn yelled at him, and Mom yelled at him, and Dad was on the verge of putting him across his knees.

After they had learned about Paul, Mom and Dad and Glenn and Judy didn't shout at him as they used to. They had learned that Paul had to be specially taught to do things. He had to be taught discipline, good behavior, and manners. Everything had to be taught to Paul carefully and with understanding. For a long while things were pretty hectic around home.

Between Moreland School and home, Paul had come along pretty well. He was thirteen now, and he was doing second-grade reading and arithmetic.

After the idea had occurred to Glenn to teach Paul to play basketball, he had mentioned it to Judy. She thought it was great. So without saying a thing to Mom, they had gone outside and started playing.

A chuckle sounded behind them. Glenn turned and saw Don Marshang and Andy Searles peering over the fence.

"Those two rookies going to play with us, Glenn?" Don wisecracked. "Or just Judy?"

"Just make sure you do all right, Mr. Marshang!" Judy answered before Glenn had a chance to. "Or maybe a rookie *will* take your place!"

"That'll be the day," Don said, and laughed. "Anyway, for a girl you throw pretty well, Judy. Too bad we can't have girls on the team."

"You're lucky you can't," Judy shot back, and looped the ball to Glenn. Glenn tossed it easily to Paul and hoped with all his heart that Paul would catch it. Paul did.

"Thataway, Paul!" Don cried. "Maybe another ten years and you'll be able to make the team!" With that, Don and Andy left.

Paul's face flushed. He gripped the ball tightly with both arms and looked sternly at Don's retreating back. "He's one guy I don't like," he muttered softly.

Judy scowled after them. "The old loudmouth," she said angrily. "Boy, would I like to see Paul make the team. What that loudmouth would say then!"

"Oh, Don's okay," Glenn said. "He just wants to be a leader in everything."

Glenn saw Mom peering through the screen door of the back porch. He grinned and waved to her. She waved back, but kept staring as if she were looking at something very strange.

"Okay. Let's shoot baskets for a while," Glenn suggested. "Throw it here, Paul. Watch how I do it."

"Okay." Paul's face brightened, as if he were glad to do something different for a change. He passed the ball to Glenn. Glenn stood in front of the basket, bounced the ball a couple of times, then shot. The first throw hit the backboard above the rim and bounced off. The second bounced back and into the net.

"Now you try it, Paul."

Glenn handed Paul the ball. Eagerly, Paul took aim and shot. The ball struck the rim, bounced off. "Oh! Missed!" he said. He tried again. This time it didn't reach as high as the rim.

"Throw it higher, Paul!" cried Glenn.

"Easy, Glenn," cautioned Judy. "You don't have to shout at him. Show him again."

Glenn showed Paul again how to stand at the foul line and shoot. He tried hard to shoot like Glenn, and little by little his throws improved.

"Thataboy, Paul!" said Glenn, smiling. "You're coming! Slow but sure!"

"I'm sinking most of them, Glenn!" Paul cried proudly. "Were you counting?"

Glenn grinned. "No, but you're doing a lot better, Paul. A lot better. Okay, let's quit. We'll practice every day. Okay? You would like to play basketball with the Sabers, wouldn't you, Paul?"

Paul's eyes brightened. "You bet!"

"Just keep practicing and you will," Glenn said.

Paul ran into the house, shouting, "Mom! Hey, Mom! Glenn and Judy are teaching me to play basketball! I'm going to play with the Sabers!"

Mom smiled and squeezed him to her, then looked at his sister and brother with a question in her eyes.

"What's going on?" she demanded softly when Paul was out of the room. "What's up those sleeves of yours?"

Judy grinned. "It's Glenn's idea, Mom. We're going to teach Paul to play basketball."

"Oh, you are?"

Glenn was grinning, too. "Basketball is good exercise, Mom. And Paul will meet a lot of guys if he plays with the Sabers. He won't just have to sit and make models and draw."

Mom's eyes grew misty. She put an arm around Glenn's shoulder. "It would do him good to get out and associate with boys more," she agreed. "He needs friends. But I don't know. It will take patience, that idea of yours. Plenty of patience."

"We know, Mom," Judy said, her eyes big and bright as plums. "But don't you think Paul can learn? Don't you really think so? That is, if we really worked with him every day?"

Mom seemed to think it over a bit, then nodded. "Of course, he can. But don't get discouraged if he takes a long time at it. Basketball is no easy game to learn, you know."

Glenn's big worry was Coach Frank Munson of the Sabers. Mr. Munson was about the toughest coach in the league. You obeyed him, or else. You hustled, or else. He wasn't going to let anyone play who didn't do his best every minute.

Last year the Sabers had finished in fifth place. You'd think the coach would have been so angry he might not want to coach anymore. But he wasn't. As a matter of fact, he had praised every member of the team for having done a good job.

"Most of you were green this year," he had said. "That's why we ended next to the cellar. Next year you'll do better. You'll see. We'll climb that ladder and maybe land on top of the heap. Just play hard, and do your best. That's all I ask."

Glenn had been one of the green ones Mr. Munson had referred to. He was still a poor passer. He had a lot to learn about basketball himself. Probably it was crazy to think that he could teach Paul basketball well enough for Paul to get on the team. If Mr. Munson wanted kids on his team who played hard every minute, what chance would Paul have? Hardly any. Maybe he should give up the idea before it was too late — before Paul might get discouraged and really become unhappy.

He mentioned this to Judy later in the evening. And right away he knew that he should not have. Her eyes flashed daggers and her lips pursed and he knew that he had just lit the fuse of a keg of dynamite.

"Oh, no, you're not going to give up now, Mr. Glenn Foster Marlette!" she exploded. "It was your idea, and it's a good one, and you and I are going to stick it out if it takes till doomsday. You hear me? Till doomsday!"

Glenn stepped back as if she might slug him. "Okay, okay," he stammered. "I was just saying it, anyway."

Her eyes quit flashing. Her lips smoothed out and curved into a warm smile.

"That's better, Glenn," she said sweetly. "Matter of fact, I knew you were just talking."

They had two weeks and three days to practice. The regular playing season began on Tuesday, November 30, according to the schedule Coach Munson had given the boys. The Sabers, as well as the other teams in the league, had already started practicing at the Recreation Hall. Games were to be played there and at the school gym.

The first week drifted by, and still Glenn didn't take Paul to the Recreation Hall to practice with the team. He wanted Paul to learn all he could about basketball at home. Even Dad worked out with them. He and Judy played against Paul and Glenn so that Paul would get the feel of competition. It wasn't much, but Glenn could see that Paul was enjoying it more than just throwing the ball back and forth and shooting at the basket.

With the opening game of the league exactly a week away, Glenn took Paul with him to the Recreation Hall. Paul took his sneakers, but Glenn was worried that Paul might not be given a uniform. The minute the coach heard that Paul had never played basketball before, he might tell Paul to go home and not waste anybody's time here. You just never knew what he might say.

The team dressed in the locker room. Paul followed Glenn like a shadow, and the guys looked at Paul as if he were someone from another planet.

They dressed in their gold, silver-trimmed uniforms, then went upstairs to the gym. Glenn's number was 12.

"Am I going to get a uniform, Glenn?" Paul asked anxiously.

"Hang on awhile," said Glenn. "I'm not sure yet. Maybe the coach doesn't have an extra one."

Boy! What a time to think about that now!

Coach Munson was already on the floor, throwing shots at the basket with Don Marshang and Andy Searles.

"About time you guys got around," he snapped as the rest of the team came running in from the basement doorway. He glanced at Paul, and frowned.

"You," he said, pointing a finger at him. "Come here a minute."

Paul, looking suddenly scared, started slowly toward him.

"Hurry! Hurry!" The coach's voice snapped like a whip.

Paul broke into a run then and stopped in front of the coach. Glenn reached Paul's side in time to hear the coach ask, "Aren't you Glenn's brother?"

Paul nodded. "Yes. My name's Paul." His eyes rolled to Glenn, then back to the coach.

"I've been teaching him basketball at home, Coach," Glenn butted in. "He's never played before."

Coach Munson's hard eyes swung toward him. "You've been teaching him? For how long?"

"Almost two weeks."

"Two weeks?" The coach looked at Paul. "You think you're good enough to play with the Sabers now, Paul? After two weeks?"

Paul shrugged. He still looked scared. "I don't know. I'd like to."

"No, he can't yet, Coach," said Glenn, suddenly embarrassed. He stared eye to eye at the coach, trying to think of how to tell the coach about Paul and why he wanted Paul to play basketball. But he couldn't tell the coach in front of Paul. You just couldn't say *those* things in front of him.

The coach smiled and put a hand on Paul's shoulder. "Tell you what. I'd be glad to have you on our team, but you do need more experience, Paul. Basketball is no easy sport. Another thing: I've got ten players now and sometimes they don't all get in." He turned to Glenn. "You know how it is, Glenn. You were on the team last year."

Glenn's jaw sagged. "Yes, but Paul . . .

well, he doesn't have to play in the games. He can just work out with us, can't he? Maybe sometime when we're far ahead . . . well, maybe *then* he can get in for a minute or so . . . I thought."

"I can catch pretty good, Coach Munson," blurted Paul hastily, his eyes glowing. "And I'm getting good at shooting baskets. Ask Glenn."

Coach Munson's lip twisted as if there were a fly on it. Then he rubbed Paul's shoulder. "Okay, Paul. I'll give you a try."

Paul's face brightened. For a second he looked as if he were going to jump with joy. "Thanks, Coach Munson!" he cried.

"Got one problem, though," added the Coach. "I don't have enough uniforms."

"He can wear mine," Glenn suggested quickly. "And I can wear my shorts."

The coach grinned. "Paul can wear his

own shorts," he said. "Okay, Paul, get back downstairs. . . ."

When Paul returned to the floor the whole Sabers team stared at him with wonder. Some of them made remarks to each other which Glenn could not hear, but which were not hard to guess. Paul Marlette on the Sabers team? Coach Munson must be nuts!

Only Benjy Myles seemed pleased to see Paul. Benjy was little for his age, but he had always played with Paul. Always, that is, until his mother had put a stop to it a year ago.

Coach Munson had the team line up in two rows, six feet apart and facing each other. Paul was at the end of one row. They passed a basketball between them. When the ball was passed to Paul he caught it. A broad, pleased grin spread across his face.

"Good!" shouted the guys.

They took turns shooting baskets from the foul line. Each took fifteen shots. Glenn sank ten. Paul missed all except two. He started to take a sixteenth shot when someone yelled.

"Hold it, Paul, boy! You've had your fifteen shots!" It was Don Marshang.

There was no mistaking the looks on the faces of Don, Andy, and some of the other guys as Paul stepped away from the foul line and handed the ball to Stevie Keester, the next in line to shoot. They weren't pleased at all that Coach Munson was allowing him to practice with them.

Glenn looked at Paul to see how Paul was taking it. Paul was taking it fine, as if he hadn't noticed those dirty looks or heard those unflattering remarks. He seemed happy to be on the team. So far it didn't seem to matter what a few of the guys were saying about him.

Finally Coach Munson picked two teams and had them scrimmage. Paul was the eleventh man and did not start. After a while the coach put him in Chet Bruner's place. Once Benjy Myles passed him the ball and Andy tried to steal it from him, but Paul hung on to it desperately for a jump ball.

"Nice going, Paul!" Glenn cried.

"Thanks, Glenn!" he answered joyously.

Practice ended and the players started downstairs to take their showers. Someone tapped Glenn on the shoulder. It was Don Marshang. Don pointed at Paul, who was several steps below them.

"Glenn, you don't expect *him* to play with us, do you?" he said, frowning. "Not *him?*"

Paul didn't improve at all during the next few days when the Sabers practiced at the Recreation Hall. One thing was noticeable, though — he was having fun. And most of the guys spoke to him when he showed up at practice and when he left. Only a few, such as Don Marshang, Andy Searles, and Stevie Keester, pretended he wasn't around. That didn't seem to bother Paul. He seemed to pretend that they weren't around, either.

That weekend, Glenn and Paul, with Judy watching them from the porch steps, practiced at home. Glenn tried to show Paul how to dribble. Paul's big difficulty was trying to dribble the ball and move it along at the same time. It wasn't easy. They also practiced passing to each other. Glenn knew he needed much improvement on passing himself, if he expected to play on the first team.

Then they used a system similar to the one the Sabers used. Glenn would shoot at the basket, run in, catch the rebound, and pass it to Paul. Paul would do the same thing. They were going well for a while.

Then Glenn, in his excitement, threw the ball hard to Paul, shouting, "Come on, Paul! Let's go!" The ball shot through Paul's hand and hit him on the face. "Ow!" he cried. A second later Glenn saw blood spurt from Paul's nose.

Paul yelled with pain, but mostly with fear, thought Glenn. He clutched his nose, saw the blood drip on it, and yelled some more.

"I'm sorry, Paul!" Glenn cried. "I'm sorry!"

He pulled off his sweatshirt and rushed to Paul's side. At the same time Judy came bounding off the steps.

"Oh, Glenn! Why weren't you more careful?" She had a wad of paper towels, which she pressed against Paul's nose. "Let's go inside, Paul. It'll be easier to take care of it in the bathroom."

"It hurts!" yelled Paul. "It hurts!"

Of all the things to happen, thought Glenn. After this Paul might get frightened whenever a pass was thrown hard at him and he'd never be able to catch it. Judy's handling him like a baby didn't help matters, either. She couldn't be around every time some accident happened to Paul, could she?

"Just a minute, Judy," he said, jumping between her and the porch steps. "Let's not take Paul inside. Do it right here. It's only a nosebleed. Didn't you ever have a nosebleed?"

"Yes, but I've never got it banged to make it bleed," she blurted. "Get out of the way."

She started to press by him, but he stepped in front of her. "We can't treat Paul like a baby, Judy. If he plays basketball he's going to get banged on the nose a dozen times, just like I have. You have to expect those things."

She stared at him. Then her eyes flashed as they always did when she got angry. "Well, what are you waiting for? Go get some ice to keep it from swelling, will you? Expect me to do everything?"

Glenn laughed, went inside, and a moment later came out with the ice. Mom had asked him what it was for, naturally. He told her, adding that it was nothing serious so that she wouldn't worry.

The bleeding stopped and Paul began

playing again as if nothing had happened. Once Glenn caught Judy's eye, and smiled. Sitting with her hands gripped around her knees, she tipped her head smartly and smiled back. He would never forget this moment. It was one of the rare occasions when he had won his way over his sister.

Tuesday rolled around. During his study periods in school Glenn thought about the game against the Gators and whether Coach Munson would have Paul suit up. So far Paul had been wearing his own shorts at the practice sessions; the team was still shy one uniform, and Coach Munson hadn't said whether he would order a uniform for Paul or not.

At five-thirty, game time, the team suited up — all except Paul, who stood silently by in the locker room.

"Sorry I don't have a uniform for you,

Paul," said the coach. "But, as I told you before, we only have ten."

"That's okay," said Paul.

But it wasn't okay, thought Glenn, sitting close by lacing his sneakers. By the sad, discouraged look on Paul's face he knew it wasn't. "Isn't he ever going to play with us, then, Coach?" he asked.

"Well, he could if one of the boys didn't show up for some reason," the coach replied.

"Don't worry about anybody not showing up," Andy Searles remarked, a broad grin on his face.

Glenn glared at him, looked again at Coach Munson. "We can take turns, can't we? I wear my uniform during the first half, and Paul wear it the second half?"

The coach smiled. "No, I don't think so, Glenn."

"How about letting him wear my uniform part of the time, Coach?" a small, husky voice said. "I don't get in the games much anyway. I didn't last year."

Glenn looked around at blond-haired, blue-eyed Benjy Myles. Benjy lived only four doors away from them, but he never came over to play anymore, not since that time almost a year ago when his mother had come after him to take him home.

"Don't you go over there to play with that boy again," Glenn had heard her say as she pulled Benjy up the sidewalk with her. "Not again. Do you understand?"

Glenn had been sitting in the shade of the large green bush, watching Benjy and Paul playing together with Paul's trucks. She hadn't seen him or she probably would not have said such a thing.

"You sure it's all right with you, Benjy?" the coach asked.

"Of course, I'm sure," said Benjy. "Paul is

a good friend of mine. He only lives four doors away from me. Don't you, Paul?"

"That's right," said Paul, and smiled.

Benjy smiled too. He really liked Paul. You could see that by the happy expression on his face and in his eyes. But what if his mother heard about it? What would she say?

"Coach," Glenn said, "I — I'd rather Paul and I changed off." He thought of an excuse at the last moment. "My uniform would fit Paul better. Benjy's is too small."

The coach looked from little Benjy to Paul, who was nearly a head taller. "Glenn's right, Benjy. Your uniform might be rather snug for Paul." He glanced at his wristwatch. "Look, we haven't got more time to discuss this now. Paul, I think it's best that you sit this game out, since we don't have a uniform for you. There are a lot of games ahead of us. I'll just have to order you a uniform. Come on. Let's get upstairs."

Paul's face dropped a mile. Glenn met his eyes and shared Paul's disappointment.

Everything seemed to crop up to keep Paul from playing.

Both teams had a brief warm-up period, taking random shots at their baskets. The referee then blew his whistle. The five starters for each team took their positions on the court. The Gators, wearing shiny green uniforms trimmed with white, looked taller than the Sabers. And stronger.

Glenn sat on the bench, Paul beside him. He felt good, even if Paul didn't. The coach had promised to get Paul a uniform.

With Andy Searles and Don Marshang at the forward positions, Frog Robbins and Stevie Keester at guard, and lanky Jim Tilton at center, the game was ready to begin.

The whistle shrilled as the referee tossed the ball up between the centers. Frog took the tap, dribbled to the side, and passed to Don. Don dribbled toward the basket, stopped in the keyhole, found a guard blocking his way, and passed to Jim. Jim broke fast for the basket, went up. Smack! The Gators' center had tried to block the layup and struck Jim's wrist. The whistle shrilled. Two shots.

Jim made the first, missed the second. The Gators caught the rebound off the boards and passed it down-court. They bounced the ball, passed it through the air, tried to work it closer to the basket. Then, from a corner, a Gator took a set shot. A clean hit!

Stevie tossed the ball from out-of-bounds to Don. Don dribbled up to the center line where he paused, then passed to Andy. Andy broke fast, then held up as a guard practically sprouted in front of him. He spun on his pivot foot, bounced a pass to Frog, and Frog took it and passed to Jim. Jim drove for the basket, went up, and laid it in.

Cheers exploded from the Sabers fans, especially from the men warming the Sabers bench. Paul was yelling, too. Glenn smiled. Paul was really enjoying the game even though he wasn't playing.

Abe Elliot and Chet Bruner went in for Frog and Stevie, and right off the bat Chet sank one from the foul line. The blond Gator forward plunked in another from the corner and their tall center made a hook shot. Both teams sank baskets and played evenly for the first four minutes. The Gators were one point ahead when Glenn went in with two minutes left in the first quarter.

He was nervous at first and nearly missed a hard pass Don Marshang shot to him. He dribbled to the side, stopped when a guard loomed in front of him. Then he heaved a pass to Jim, who was standing in the clear down in the corner. Jim caught it, jumped and turned in the same movement, and shot. In!

The Sabers went ahead, 13 to 12, but couldn't hold on to the lead. When the quarter ended they trailed, 15 to 13.

In the second quarter Glenn hurled a pass to Andy. A fast Gator forward intercepted it, dribbled all the way down-court, and sank it for two points. The Sabers hit for more baskets but could not overcome the Gators, who seemed to match every basket with one of their own. The quarter was three minutes old when Glenn caught a pass from Jim and was fouled. One shot.

He stood at the free-throw line and hoped desperately that he would make it. The Gators led by two points. To decrease that lead by one would not help much, but it would mean a lot to him. Paul would like it.

He caught the toss from the referee, bounced the ball a couple of times, looked at the basket, and shot. The ball struck the backboard, bounced back against the rim, then rolled off the side. Something like a heavy ball hit the pit of his stomach. What lousy luck.

Jim and the Gators' center scrambled for the rebound. Both got it, struggled for it, and the whistle blew for a jump ball.

Seconds later Stevie sank one from ten feet away. The Gators evened it up. Both teams played tight ball till the horn sounded, ending the first half.

Once in the third quarter the Sabers managed to catch up with the Gators. And before the quarter ended Andy sank a foul shot to put the Sabers ahead. The fans grew more excited as the minutes wore on. At times the Gators seemed to outplay the Sabers. They grabbed the rebounds and got the ball hurriedly down into the Sabers zone. But the Sabers defense, all grouped in a close area under the basket, kept the Gators from coming in for an easy shot. With only a few minutes to go, the Gators were playing cautiously. They weren't taking crazy shots as they were before. They wanted to make sure each shot counted. The score was in their favor, 44–42.

"Get that ball!" Coach Munson shouted from the bench. "Get that ball!"

Then the blond boy took a set from the corner. The ball arched through the air, sank through the hoop with scarcely a whisper. 46–42!

Don called for a time out. Coach Munson sent in Glenn, took out Stevie. The look Don gave Glenn as he trotted in was all but friendly.

Glenn was in half a minute when he caught a pass from Andy near the basket, took a jump shot — and made it! The fans roared. Even Don slapped him on the back, which surprised Glenn. As he ran toward the other end of the court he took a quick glance at Paul. Paul was clapping like crazy.

The seconds skipped by quickly. Benjy, in for Andy, was fouled almost instantly. He was given two shots. He sank the first, missed the second. The Sabers crawled to within a point of tying the score, but could go no further. They were squeezed out, 49 to 48.

On Thursday, December 2, the Sabers tangled with the Cowboys. Last Tuesday the Cowboys had lost their opener to the Shawnees, so both the Sabers and the Cowboys were looking for their first win.

Glenn received his first shock of the evening when Coach Munson called off his name as one of the starters. He was taking Frog's place at left guard.

Don Marshang was hot almost from the instant the ball was tossed up between the centers. He plunked in a jump shot from the keyhole and a few seconds later stole the ball from a Cowboy, dribbled it all the way up-court, and sank a layup. The red glass knobs on the scoreboard kept changing on the Sabers' side, while nothing showed on the Cowboys' side. It was 10 to 0 when the Cowboys had the ball and their coach signaled their captain to call for time out.

Both teams went to their respective benches. While the coach of the Cowboys began telling his charges what their trouble was, the coach of the Sabers looked at his team with a happy gleam in his eyes.

"You guys are popping them in like you know what you're doing," he said proudly. "Why didn't you play like that in the first game?"

"We didn't play the Cowboys the first game," Stevie answered soberly.

"Oh. A comedian. Okay. But make sure you don't get spurred."

Everyone laughed. They sure felt good.

Glenn wiped his face with a towel. He looked at Paul sitting on the bench next to Benjy. Seeing the two together made him think of that incident a year ago when Benjy's mother had come to take Benjy home. Here on the basketball court was the first time that the two boys had been together since then.

"Glenn — Stevie, take a rest," advised the coach. "Frog — Benjy, report."

A broad smile crossed Paul's face. "Thataboy, Benjy! Sink a couple for me!"

Good thing he doesn't get discouraged sitting on the bench, thought Glenn. Maybe watching the game and getting excited about it made him forget that he wasn't playing.

Time was up. The Cowboys took the ball from out-of-bounds, passed to their front court. Their tall center bolted toward the basket, caught a pass, leaped up with it. His easy shot against the boards went in for the Cowboys' first field goal.

Benjy tried a jump shot from a corner, was fouled when a short, redheaded kid bumped into him.

"Two shots!" yelled the referee, and signaled the offender's number to the scorekeeper.

"Thataway, Benj!" Glenn shouted. "Sink 'em both, kid!"

Paul clapped and shouted, too. He was all for little Benjy Myles.

Benjy stepped to the free-throw line, accepted the ball from the referee, and measured the basket with a long, steady look. He didn't hold the ball up in front of his chest as many foul shooters did. He held it low. Carefully he tossed it up. The ball arched sharply — dropped in!

"Nice shot, Benjy!" cried Paul, clapping as hard as he could.

Benjy took his second shot. He made that too! The fans cheered and whistled. Especially Paul. Glenn looked at the faces in the crowd, wondering if Benjy's parents were among them. He didn't see them, and was sure they weren't. Benjy's father was a salesman and wasn't home half the time. And Benjy's mother never went to sporting events, not in winter nor in summer. Anyway, Glenn had never seen her at them.

The Cowboys had a lucky streak and sank three baskets. Then Don took a long shot from the center line just before the first quarter buzzer sounded, and made it.

The Cowboys had better luck the second quarter. Their two scrappy forwards, who were brothers, began dropping in baskets from the corners, and it seemed that the Sabers were unable to do a thing about it.

When the half ended the Cowboys had gotten to within one point of tying the score. It was 20–19.

In the third quarter Glenn tried to stop a player from shooting a layup and struck the player's hand instead of the ball. It was Glenn's second foul of the game. This time it meant more than it did the first time. It gave the Cowboys a chance to creep ahead.

Disappointed, Glenn walked toward the center line, holding up one hand to identify himself to the scorekeeper, and waited for the Cowboy to take his two shots.

Both went in and the Cowboys were ahead, 21–20.

"Come on, Glenn!" Don said, tapping him on the hip. "Let's get 'em back!"

No one was more anxious to get those points back than Glenn. He guarded his man like a hawk, shifting with him as if he were the man's shadow. The Cowboys were near the Sabers basket, trying desperately to put in another one.

A pass shot like a comet to Glenn's right side. He intercepted it, and dribbled it toward the center line where two Cowboys tried to take it from him. He saw Jim swing around behind him, and pushed the ball between his legs to the tall center. Jim scooped it up and dribbled it all the way up-court. The fans cheered and screamed as Jim laid it up.

Glenn felt better. Jim got the cheers, but it was he, Glenn, who had passed him the ball. He didn't let up. He continued to guard his man closely, hoping that he might be able to intercept another pass. But the Cowboys seemed to play more cautiously now. They were making more sure of their passes.

The referee's whistle shrilled. "Traveling!"

he cried, indicating the violation by rotating his hands. The ball went to the Sabers.

Glenn passed it from out-of-bounds to Andy, then ran down the sideline. Andy passed it back to him. He tried to take a shot, but his guard sprang like a cat in front of him. Glenn saw Don waving on the opposite side and pegged the ball to him. The instant he let it go he knew the throw was wild. It sailed far over Don's head and into the bleachers where one of the fans caught it.

That was his big trouble — throwing passes. The horn honked and Dan Levine, a tall blond boy, came in and replaced him.

"Shooting for the moon, Glenn?" Coach Munson's grin wasn't too pleasant. "Don't throw to a man a mile away from you. Wait'll your passes are more accurate."

Glenn nodded. He knew that was his

trouble, but he usually didn't think about it in time.

The third quarter ended with the Sabers leading by a thin margin, 36–35. The coach sent in two guys to replace Jim and Don, and for a moment the spot on Glenn's left side was vacant. Paul came and sat beside him.

"Sure wish I was playing," he muttered softly.

"Don't worry," said Glenn. "Coach Munson will get you a uniform. Maybe he'll have it by the next game." He smiled. "It's a lot of fun, isn't it?"

"I think I could do as good as some of them," Paul said.

Glenn laughed. "Well, it looks easy. But it isn't. You'll see. The thing is, you can't let stuff bother you. If you miss shots, you can't get sick over it. Or if you throw a bad pass like I did, you just try to do better the next time. You'll understand after you play awhile."

"If I ever play," Paul said, discouraged.

"Don't worry. You will," Glenn assured him.

It was nip and tuck all the way to the very last minute when the Sabers really got hot and dumped in three baskets in rapid order. They won 48 to 41, sending the Cowboys home with their second loss in a row.

No teams practiced on Fridays, so Glenn took Paul with him to the Recreation Hall and they practiced on foul shots. Paul had trouble finding his range for a while. As soon as he did he began hitting baskets almost fifty percent of the time. They had to quit when a bunch of kids came and wanted the court.

The next morning they practiced foul shots and layups at home. It was Saturday, and the sun was out bright and warm. Only small patches of snow lingered here and there on the lawn. The blacktop driveway was clear.

Benjy came and stood watching them from the sidewalk until Paul invited him to join them. Glenn was surprised to see Benjy there, but said nothing. He knew that the two liked to play together and enjoyed each other's company.

After a while Judy came out and played with them. Later, she and Glenn watched Paul shoot baskets from a foul line which Glenn had drawn with white chalk. Paul started off by missing the first few, then began sinking them better and better.

"Hey, you're doing great," Benjy said, smiling.

"I'm going to be an expert," Paul said, "if it takes me a million years!"

Judy nudged Glenn. “Glenn, wouldn’t it be funny if Paul did become an expert?”

“At foul shooting?” Glenn shrugged. “He probably could if that’s all he did. But basketball isn’t only foul shooting.”

“I know. But many times foul shots make a big difference in a game, don’t they?”

“Yes. But with Paul . . .” Glenn paused. “He just won’t play that much. But he could get good at it. I guess he could get real good if he did it a lot.”

A voice spoke up behind them — a woman’s voice, with a familiar ring to it.

“Benjy! Ben — jy! Do you hear me?” It was sweet and singsongish.

Glenn and Judy turned. Mrs. Myles was standing on the sidewalk, a smile on her lips as sweet as her voice. A dark-brown fur coat was draped over her shoulders.

“Coming, Mom!” Benjy said, and dashed

out of the yard. "So long, Paul — Glenn — Judy! See you Tuesday!"

"Right," said Glenn, then watched Mrs. Myles take Benjy's hand and propel him hastily up the street, as if they had to get away from there or else. Suddenly she wasn't the sweet-voiced, sweet-smiling mother anymore. She was blurting out something to Benjy, but they were too far away for Glenn to hear what she said.

Glenn turned and saw that Paul had stopped throwing at the basket. He was watching, too.

It wasn't until after dinner that Glenn and Judy mentioned the incident to Mom and Dad. Paul was outside again, shooting baskets.

"Why won't she let Benjy play with him?" Glenn asked, bewilderedly. "I don't get it, Mom. Paul's a good kid. What's she afraid of?"

Mom took a deep breath, as if the question had no easy answer. Dad and Judy had just finished doing the dishes. They were all sitting in the living room, watching the news on TV.

"I heard that Mrs. Myles won't let Benjy play with Paul because she's afraid Benjy will get just like Paul," Judy said.

Glenn stared at her. "Who told you that?"

"One of the girls in school. Her mother heard Mrs. Myles say that. Isn't that ridiculous?"

"It's worse than ridiculous," replied Mom, and for a moment her eyes blazed. "I hope that someday Mrs. Myles will realize how wrong she is for thinking that way. If she'd only take a little interest she'd find out that there are many families with a disabled child growing up with brothers and sisters, and things like that never happen. Take our own family. Both of you are doing fine. Does having a brother who is less fortunate than you make you disabled, too?"

"Mrs. Hotshot Myles had better do some reading up on the subject before she makes any more statements like that," Dad broke in angrily.

"You'd be surprised at the number of people who feel the same way," said Mom.

"I know," replied Dad. "They want to keep away from such kids because they're afraid of what the kids might say or do. Can you imagine? It's the worst thing in the world to avoid the child that way. He needs love and understanding even more than other children do. You two kids have noticed that. You've seen how happy Paul is when we all chip in and show him our affection. We correct him when he makes mistakes, praise him when he does something well. We've tried to use patience with Paul, and I think we've come a long way. Right, Corinne?"

"I'm sure we have," Mom said.

"I'm sure we have, too," said Judy. "He

still gets angry sometimes when I try to correct him, but it only lasts a minute. And he appreciates praise. The thing is, will he learn more as he gets older? Do you think he'll be able to get a job when he gets in his twenties?"

"Of course he'll learn more," answered Mom. "Not much, and not quickly. But there can be jobs available for him when he gets in his twenties. That magazine we subscribe to mentions such jobs all the time."

"The important period is now," Dad said, forgetting the news for a while. "During his teenage years. Kids his age are going places in small groups — ball games, movies, swimming. They won't take Paul because he can't keep up with them. It makes him a social outcast. That's why now is the most important time in Paul's life. We must help him all we can. You kids have come up with a great idea by having Paul learn basketball."

The subject changed to Christmas, which was only a few weeks away. What could he get Paul for a present, Glenn wanted to know.

Shirts and pajamas, Mom suggested. What about Plasticine models, Glenn asked. Paul enjoyed making things with Plasticine. That was fine, Mom agreed.

"What are you and Dad going to get for him, Mom?"

Mom smiled. "That'll be a surprise," she said.

Paul enjoyed playing with toys. But Glenn and Paul had all sorts of trucks. Glenn had a freight train set which Paul enjoyed playing with, too. There really wasn't much else he could get Paul.

It started to snow late that afternoon. By

morning it stopped, leaving about three inches of snow on the ground.

On Sunday they slept late, had a big brunch — pancakes, sausages, and scrambled eggs — then the three children shoveled the snow off the driveway and played basketball. Later Judy went to visit one of her girlfriends, and Glenn went inside to watch the Eagles-Colts game on television. He wasn't especially crazy about watching it. It got tiresome sitting there very long. He couldn't figure out how Dad could sit there watching a whole game. As a matter of fact, Dad could sit and watch two full games in a row.

The game was still in the first quarter when Glenn heard voices yelling out front. He stepped to the window and saw three boys throwing snowballs as fast as they could make them. They were throwing them at Paul.

“Those meatheads!” Glenn snarled, and crossed the floor to put on his coat and hat.

“What’s going on?” asked Dad.

“Some wise guys are ganging up on Paul,” said Glenn. “I’m going out there and help him. If they want a snow fight, we’ll give it to ’em.”

Dad shrugged, smiled, and returned to his business. Glenn put on his coat, hat, and boots, and hurried out. A big smile came over Paul’s face as he saw Glenn. He was spattered all over with snow.

“Come on, Glenn!” he shouted enthusiastically. “Let’s give it to ’em!”

The snowballs came flying. One struck Glenn on the shoulder and spattered as he bent over to scoop up a handful of the white stuff. Quickly he made it into a ball, fired it, scooped up another handful, fired again, and hit a target. Now and then Paul’s shots hit home, too, and he would shout happily.

Frog Robbins came by and joined Glenn and Paul. In a few moments the other three boys had enough. They laughed, brushed the snow off their coats, and left.

"Thanks for the help, Frog!" Paul said. "Guess we won that fight, didn't we?"

Frog grinned. "We sure did."

Glenn invited Frog in to watch the football game. Frog accepted. After a while Glenn noticed that Paul wasn't around, although the three boys had come into the house together. He was certain that Paul hadn't gone out again.

Glenn went to the room that he and Paul shared and saw Paul at the desk. He was drawing a picture.

"What have you got there?" Glenn asked.

Paul looked at him with a proud gleam in his eye. He held up the picture. There were two figures in it that looked like people leaning into a strong wind. There was a house at the side of the picture and a tree bending from the wind. The entire sheet was covered with circles deeply impressed in the paper, coming down in a slant.

"It's snowing!" Paul explained, a glow on his face. "Snowing hard!"

Glenn nodded. So that was what the heavy circles meant.

"Say, Paul, that's good," he said. "That's really good."

"Thanks!" said Paul. He was smiling broadly, proud of his drawing, and pleased that Glenn had told him it was good.

Glenn walked out of the room, wondering just how he would have drawn a picture of snow snowing hard.

In the locker room just before the game with the Shawnees, Coach Munson approached Paul. He was holding one hand behind him. From where Glenn sat he saw that the hand held a blue box. A warm, prickly feeling rippled over him. The coach had Paul's uniform.

"Bring your sneakers with you?" the coach asked Paul.

A smile flickered over Paul's face. He stuck out his right foot. "Got 'em on," he said.

"Good." The coach handed Paul the box. "Here's your uniform. Get into it. Maybe we'll get you in the game for a while tonight."

Paul's eyes grew as wide and bright as Christmas-tree bulbs. He took the box, yanked off the cover, and lifted out the brand-new gold-colored jersey. The coach held up one side of it so that the number could be seen. It was 22.

"Thanks, Coach!" Paul cried. "It looks sharp!"

In his excitement he tried to undress too quickly, but only fumbled with the buttons of his shirt and wasn't getting anywhere.

"Take your time!" Glenn said, laughing. "No one's going to leave you here alone. Let me help you."

He helped Paul remove his shirt and then started his jersey on for him. Paul was beaming. "He got me the uniform, Glenn!" he said enthusiastically. "He kept his word, didn't he?"

"Yes, he did, Paul," Glenn answered, his heart singing as he knew Paul's must be too. "Coach Munson always keeps his word."

Paul finished dressing by himself. When they walked up on the court Paul strutted across the floor like a proud rooster. *Look at him,* Glenn thought. *Right now he's the happiest guy in the world.*

Glenn didn't get in the game until the second quarter. Two minutes before it was over the coach sent in Paul in place of Stevie Keester. It was Paul's first experience in a real game. He didn't run much. He looked nervous. He just kept following close to his man as Coach Munson had told him to do.

Several times the Shawnee made a fast break, getting away from Paul and catching a pass with no one around him. At one time the man went in for a layup. The second time he tried it Glenn rushed in and the Shawnee's try for a basket missed. The crowd shouted for Glenn. Paul stayed in till the horn sounded, ending the first half.

The Sabers had a good lead, 26–17. With one minute to go in the third quarter Paul went in again. Right away he ran into his man unexpectedly and a foul was called on him. A little while later he committed another foul — holding. The Shawnees gained a point when the fouled player sank the shot.

The coach took Paul out. "Can't hold on a guy, Paul," the coach warned him. "Just keep your arms in front of him. Don't touch him."

Paul nodded. He looked hurt. He had seemed to be having so much fun. Now, all of a sudden, he had caused two fouls and was yanked. All the fun was gone out of him.

The Sabers outplayed the Shawnees all the way through. Every player, except Paul, put in almost equal time. The Shawnees simply couldn't do much. They lost to the Sabers, 51–36.

Paul forgot about the fouls. He was happy again. In the dressing room, and on their way home, there was no boy more thrilled than he. Glenn was thrilled, too, because Paul was. Their enthusiasm was shared by Mom, Dad, and Judy, all of whom had gone to the game.

"You did fine, Paul," Dad said, his arm around Paul's shoulder, squeezing him tightly. "You did just fine."

"Didn't make any baskets, though," Paul said.

"That's all right," remarked Glenn. "I made only two. There are other guys who can do the shooting. You just learn to guard your man so *he* doesn't make baskets. Right, Dad?"

"Right." Dad smiled. "And Paul was doing a pretty good job of it, too."

Glenn looked over the crowd moving slowly through the hall to the exit door. He spotted someone he least expected, and his eyes almost popped — Mrs. Myles!

It was the first game she had ever attended. Perhaps it was because it was the second game of the doubleheader (the 5:30 game had been between the Gators and the Blue Waves). And it was almost eight o'clock, which was sort of late for Benjy to be out. Or perhaps she wanted to make sure Benjy didn't walk home with a certain boy.

"Hey, Glenn, seen Stevie?"

It was Jim Tilton, their center. "He was with Frog and Andy," said Glenn.

Jim nodded and threaded his way through

the crowd. Nothing was said about Paul's playing. Not one guy had said a single word about Paul. To them he's just an invisible man, Glenn thought with a heavy heart. Well, playing had made Paul feel happier. Even a little happier is better than nothing.

They played the Jackrabbits on Thursday. The Jackrabbits rolled into the lead right away and held it throughout the first half. Glenn was in a few minutes and pumped in two baskets and two foul shots for a total of six points.

In the second half the Jackrabbits kept up their hot streak. Toward the end of the third quarter Don Marshang started to drive and sank three baskets. Twice he was fouled and both times sank his shots. By the middle of the fourth quarter the Sabers were neck to neck with the Jackrabbits, and the small crowd was in pandemonium.

Glenn got in with three minutes to go.

He had played half of the third quarter and hadn't scored. He caught a pass from Frog and dribbled it to the front court, saw Stevie open and passed. Stevie tried to drive, stopped as two men surged on him. Glenn swept around his guard and headed toward the baseline near the basket. Stevie passed to him. Glenn caught it, leaped for a jump shot. Made it! Sabers — 55; Jackrabbits — 53.

The seconds ticked on. The Jackrabbits tied it up. Jim sank a long one to put the Sabers ahead again. With two minutes to go, the Jackrabbits, now in possession of the ball, played more cautiously. They wanted to get the ball as near to the basket as possible before they shot.

They worked it in. Their tall center drove, leaped for a shot. It missed! Jim caught the rebound, passed to Stevie. With a fast break they got the ball to their front court.

"Freeze it! Freeze it!" came the shouts from the fans.

There was less than a minute to play. The seconds were ticking away. The crowd was getting more and more excited.

"Take that ball away from them!" a Jackrabbit fan yelled.

The Jackrabbits, playing a tight man-to-man defense, pressed too hard. Don Marshang, who had the ball, was pushed and given a one-and-one shot. He made the first, missed the second. The Jackrabbits caught the rebound, bolted down-court with the ball, drove for a layup, missed.

For a while there was wild excitement as again and again Jackrabbits' hands went up to tap the ball into the basket. The ball just wouldn't go in. The game went to the Sabers, 58–55.

It wasn't until the teams headed for their

showers that Glenn realized that Paul hadn't played in the game at all.

Paul played for a minute of the second quarter in the game against the Blue Waves on Tuesday. Not once did a Saber throw him the ball. But when the Blue Waves were in possession of it, Paul watched his man like a hawk. He was getting better, Glenn told himself, in spite of what the others thought.

Glenn played most of the third quarter, sinking two baskets and one foul shot. But he had three fouls on him and began to get cautious. Two more fouls and he'd be out.

Dan Levine was in for him when the fourth quarter got under way. After two minutes of play Coach Munson took Stevie out and put in Paul.

"I just like to have him in there for a while to get him used to playing," the coach said to Glenn. "He's still awfully slow catching on.

But as long as he's in there even a little bit now and then I think he's happy, don't you?"

Glenn smiled. The coach had never said anything to him about Paul before. "He sure is," Glenn said.

"Probably talks about it at home, doesn't he?"

"He sure does. The only thing —" Glenn paused. He wished suddenly he hadn't started to say something else.

The coach looked at him. "The only thing what?"

Glenn shrugged. "Oh, nothing."

"Come on, out with it. What were you going to say?"

Glenn's voice faltered. "Well, I was hoping the guys would be different."

The coach nodded. "I know what you mean, Glenn. Just be patient. Give them time. They'll come around."

There was a wild scramble under the

Sabers basket. Glenn took a quick look at the score. Sabers — 47; Blue Waves — 49. Man, it was close.

"Get that rebound!" Coach Munson shouted. "Get that rebound!"

Glenn looked for Paul. Excitement flamed up in him as he saw Paul under the basket with the rest of them, trying to catch the ball.

And then he did get it! He leaped, shot, and the ball went in!

"Oh, no!" Coach Munson moaned, and covered his eyes with his hands.

Everyone on the Sabers bench, and the remaining four on the floor, and all those Sabers fans moaned, too.

Paul had shot the ball into the wrong basket.

Coach Munson removed Paul from the game and sent in another player. Glenn was glad that it wasn't him the coach was sending in. His heart was beating like crazy. Paul had sure goofed. He had given the Blue Waves two points, putting them four points ahead.

Paul sat beside Glenn. His eyes were dim.

"Don't cry, Paul!" Glenn said huskily into his ear. "For crying out loud, don't do that! It was just a mistake!"

"Don Marshang yelled at me," Paul said,

his voice ready to crack. "He called me a birdbrain."

That doggone Marshang. If anybody was a birdbrain, it was him.

"Don Marshang doesn't know any better," said Glenn. He picked up the towel lying near his feet. "Here. Dry yourself."

A little while later the coach had him go in for Dan Levine. *I'm going to make up for Paul's goof,* Glenn promised himself. He played hard, covering his man like a tent. His chance came. He intercepted a pass, dribbled it to the center line, passed to Don. Don passed to Jim. Jim dribbled across the keyhole, flipped a pass to Glenn, who was running in. Glenn took it, leaped, just as a hand smacked his wrist.

The whistle shrilled as the ball wiggled through the net. The referee signaled to the scorekeeper that the basket counted, and that the foul was on 42.

"Thataway, Glenn!" Paul shouted from the bench.

He made the foul shot, and cheers burst from the Sabers fans. *I got back those two points and one extra,* Glenn thought. *But we're still one behind.*

He never played as hard as he did those last remaining moments. He had another opportunity to shoot, and missed the ring by inches. Don tried his best to sink a field goal, too. But the Blue Waves swarmed over the Sabers like hornets. The seconds dribbled away until there were no more left. The Blue Waves edged out the Sabers, 51–50.

Don, Andy, and Stevie had no words to say to anyone in the locker room. No good words, that was. "If that birdbrain hadn't given them that basket we would've taken them," Don said to Andy. He said it softly, but Glenn, sitting only a few feet away, heard him.

His neck grew hot. He looked up at Don, but Don was unlacing his sneakers and didn't lift his eyes.

As they left the Recreation Hall for home Paul couldn't get over the mistake he had made. "I thought it was our basket! I wouldn't have shot if I didn't think so, Glenn! I thought it was —"

"Forget it," said Glenn. "I told you anybody could make a mistake like that, didn't I? And for crying out loud, don't cry!"

"Patience, Glenn," said Judy, who had been walking on Paul's other side and now squeezed in between them.

Glenn shook his head and crunched his teeth. Patience. Sometimes it was just too hard to hang on to.

The next day somebody started to spread

the news around school that the coach wasn't going to let Paul play again. It seemed as if everyone in the whole Livingston School had learned that Paul Marlette had shot the ball into the wrong basket last night. You'd think he had committed the crime of the century.

On Thursday the Sabers played the Gators and Glenn began to wonder if the rumor was true, that Paul wasn't going to play. But Paul was there in uniform, tall and proud as if nothing had happened.

The Gators were trampling over the Sabers like giants. They led 32 to 19 going into the second half, and Glenn was beginning to believe that Paul wasn't going to play regardless.

But with two minutes to go in the final quarter, and the Gators still far in the lead, Coach Munson took out Benjy and put in Paul. Paul stayed with his man most of those two minutes. Once he committed a foul. But the important thing was that he played. All that gossip in school was as false as a Halloween mask.

In the Cowboys game on December 21, Paul played a minute in the first quarter and two minutes in the second. Glenn played most of both quarters and chalked up four baskets and two foul shots for ten points. The Sabers piled it on the Cowboys again in the second half, and in each quarter Paul played a little. Twice he caught a rebound and passed the ball back to a teammate.

No one said a thing about Paul's catching the rebound the first time except Glenn. "Nice going, Paul," he said simply. After the second rebound Paul caught, Stevie said, "Thataway, Paul! You're coming along fine!"

Paul's face brightened as if a candle had been lit inside him.

* * *

The next evening Dad, the boys, and Judy drove out and bought a Christmas tree. School had been let out at noon for the Christmas holidays. The kids didn't have to return until the first week of January. Paul's vacation from Moreland School was at the same time.

They put up the tree and decorated it that night. Most of the presents had already been bought and wrapped. The boys hauled in the presents from the various rooms and Judy placed them under the tree on top of the white tissue paper she first had laid carefully underneath.

There was one more thing Mom said she had to get, but she wouldn't tell what it was. Nor for whom.

On Thursday, two days before Christmas, the Sabers played the Shawnees. Don Marshang and some of the other guys thought that it would be a runaway for the Sabers, since they had already beaten the Shawnees once. During the first quarter it began to look as if Don's prediction was right. The Sabers were pumping in the ball from all over the front court.

Then the Shawnees, who were playing a zone defense, changed to a man-to-man. The bright numbers on the scoreboard began to change. Paul fouled a Shawnee as the player was about to lay one in. The ball missed the basket, but the player was given two shots. He made them both.

Less than thirty seconds later Paul accidentally tripped a Shawnee dribbling the ball for his second foul. The Shawnee was given a shot and made it. Paul was taken out. Glenn could see that even the coach's soft talk wasn't helping Paul's cheerless attitude.

Paul got in just for a minute in the second half. He intercepted a pass from a Shawnee that surprised him more than anyone else. Then what did he do but throw it wildly across the court, intending it for Stevie. The pass was so high it sailed into the crowd.

The coach yanked him and Paul didn't get in again.

"He was worse tonight than he's ever been, Judy," Glenn told her at home. She had too bad a cold to go see the game. Only Dad had gone with the boys. "And I thought he was getting better."

"I told you to be patient," she said. "Rome wasn't built in a day, you know."

Just then he heard a noise from another part of the house. "What was that?"

Judy rose to her elbow on the couch, her eyes wide as bottle caps. "Sounded like it came from Paul's room," she said worriedly.

"I think it did," Dad said.

He and Glenn rushed to Paul's room. Paul was standing before his desk, gripping something very tightly in his hand. It was a model of a boy he had made a long time ago. A part of it was in his hand, a part of it on the floor, as if he had banged it against the edge of the desk.

"I didn't play good tonight, did I?" he cried, his eyes blurring. "I didn't play good at all!"

Glenn's heart suddenly ached. He knew how Paul felt. He knew exactly. "So who played good?" he said. "Nobody did."

Dad hugged Paul gently. "There, now," he said. "Take it easy. Like Glenn said, no one really played too well. That's basketball. Even those boys who play a lot have many bad nights, too. Forget it, son. Just try to do better next time, that's all."

"The guys think I — I'll never play good," Paul sobbed. "They — they all think that way."

"I don't," said Dad.

"Neither do I," said Glenn. "You'll get good, Paul. You wait and see. Then you can show those guys."

Paul blinked away the tears. He pulled a tissue from a box by his bed and blew his nose.

"I know you don't, Glenn," he stammered. "And you either, Dad. And Benjy."

"Benjy's a nice kid," Glenn said, and cracked a smile.

Dad picked up the piece from the floor. "Come on," he said. "Let's put that model back together again, shall we?"

Paul dried his eyes and started to put the pieces back together. He did it very carefully, while Glenn and Dad watched. Glenn's heart still ached, but not as much as it did before.

'TWAS the night before Christmas, when all through the house
Not a creature was stirring, not even a mouse;
The stockings were hung by the chimney with care,
In hopes that Saint Nicholas soon would be there . . .

Dad's voice was the only sound in the stillness of the house as he read the poem that he always read on Christmas Eve. He was sitting in one of the easy chairs, Mom in the other. The three children were sitting on the sofa, listening to every word. Glenn had memorized parts of it so that he was able to say them silently with Dad.

The blue, red, and orange lights on the tree shone on their faces. Lighted blue bulbs framed the picture window. The starry night was like a blue-black cardboard speckled with holes.

Dad finished the poem, folded the book, and put it aside. "Well, it's time for bed," he said.

"Daddy, I think you do a terrific job reading that poem," Judy said, the lights on the tree shining in her eyes. "I don't think this would seem like a complete Christmas Eve if you didn't read it."

"Why, thank you, daughter." Dad smiled. "I rather feel the same way."

Glenn said good night and headed for his room. He saw a new package beside the others under the tree. It was large. He glanced at the tag on it. *To Paul. From Mom and Dad.*

They rose early the next morning and walked to church. It was so crowded many people stood at the rear and sides. Reverend Thomas gave a fine Christmas sermon. At dismissal, he wished all of them a happy Christmas and said he'd see most of them again next Sunday and the others next Christmas.

They returned home. Mom made coffee for herself and Dad, while the kids ate cereal and milk. She had a ham cooking in the oven and was going to make a big dinner.

Afterwards Judy passed out the gifts. Most of them were things to wear — socks, sweaters, pajamas. Glenn also received two large books on the stars and planets and a model of a spacecraft. And Paul got a Plasticine model set. But it was the large box that made everyone curious. Everyone, that is, except Mom and Dad.

Paul's face was eager as he fumbled with the wrapper. He uncovered a large box, lifted the lid, looked in. On either side of him Judy and Glenn peered curiously too.

"It's a keyboard!" Judy cried.

"A keyboard? For me? Oh, boy!" He flung himself at Mom and Dad and hugged them both. Then he looked bewildered. "But how do you play a keyboard?"

"I'll teach you." Mom smiled. "Lift it out, dear."

Dad lifted the keyboard out of the box. It was a beautiful shiny instrument, equipped with a music stand and legs.

Glenn stared perplexedly. "Think Paul will learn to play it?" he asked. It sure seemed as if Mom and Dad had gone too far this time. They didn't really expect Paul to learn to play that keyboard, did they?

"I think he will," said Mom confidently.

She placed a chair in front of the keyboard and sat down. Then she picked up some literature that came with the instrument and two small paper boxes. One contained cutout letters which she pressed against the keys. The other contained a metronome, an instrument that kept time. Mom wound it up and the slender metal rod inside began clicking back and forth. Mom placed the metronome on the keyboard. She opened a songbook to "Jingle Bells."

"See those letters above each note, Paul?" said Mom. "Watch closely. Just press the keys that match the letters. That's all there is to it."

Mom played the song all the way through, then let Paul take over. He played very slowly. Mom helped by holding a finger above the letter on the music. As he played, a rosy glow brightened Paul's cheeks.

He will learn to play it! Glenn thought, his heart singing. *He will!*

After dinner Paul came out of his room, dressed in his winter clothes.

Glenn was reading one of his books on the stars and planets. He glanced up. "Hey, where are you going?"

"I got a present for Benjy," answered Paul. "I'm going to take it to him."

Glenn frowned. "Why? Did he give you a present?"

"No." The smile faded from Paul's face. "It's a top. He likes tops."

"But you know how his mother is," said Glenn. "She's awful funny. Why don't you wait? If he gets you something, then give him the top. If he doesn't, keep it yourself."

Paul looked at him awhile, undecided. At last he turned and walked back to his room.

Glenn pressed his lips firmly together and shook his head. Was it right telling Paul what he had? He wasn't sure. Boy, that old Mrs. Myles really made things rough at times.

Paul came out of his room, his winter clothes still on. "Want to come out and play basketball awhile, Glenn?" he asked.

The stuff about planets was interesting, and Glenn hated to break away from it. But he had lots of time to read those books. "Okay, Paul. I'll get my coat."

"I'll shovel the snow off the driveway," said Paul happily, and walked out.

They played till dusk.

The next afternoon Don Marshang, Andy Searles, and a group of other guys — some from other basketball teams — stopped by while Glenn and Paul were shooting foul shots. Don asked Glenn if he'd like to go along with them to the Recreation Hall to play basketball. They were going to choose up sides.

"Yes, I'll come along," Glenn said. "Okay if Paul comes too?"

"Sure. Bring —" one of the guys started to say.

"Why?" interrupted Don. "We need only one more man. Come on, Glenn. Paul can work on his foul shots."

Glenn felt funny leaving Paul alone.

"Come on, before somebody else gets there and takes over the court," Don said, and started to lead off with the gang.

Glenn started after them. He turned just before he was past the house and saw Paul holding the ball in his hands, looking at him. Glenn stopped. His heart was pounding.

"I've changed my mind," he said. "I don't think I'll go."

"Why can't he bring Paul?" a guy started to say again.

"Never mind!" Don barked. "We don't

need him nor that —" He broke off and gazed at Glenn with cold, steely eyes.

Glenn's fists were clenched. "You'd better not say it, Don!" he cried hotly. "You'd just better not say it!"

The Sabers played the Jackrabbits on the following Tuesday. Glenn hadn't seen Don since Sunday. He wondered how Don was going to act. Was Don so sore that he'd never pass the ball to Glenn again?

The Jackrabbits took the lead right away. Glenn played the last two minutes of the first quarter and found that what he had expected was right. There were times Don could have passed the ball to him but didn't.

Coach Munson let Glenn start the second quarter. It was the Jackrabbits' ball. They tossed it in from out-of-bounds. With short passes they moved it to their front court. As they crossed the center line Don streaked in — intercepted the ball! Suddenly two Jackrabbits swarmed around him. Glenn was open.

"Here, Don!" he cried.

Don feinted a pass to him, but didn't throw. A moment later one of the Jackrabbits knocked the ball out of Don's hands. There was a frantic scramble for the ball. The whistle shrilled.

"Jump!" yelled the referee.

Glenn caught Don's eye, and Don looked away.

Don outjumped his man, tapped the ball to Andy. Andy barely got it away from an opponent, started to dribble it up-court, then passed to Frog. Frog crossed the center line, passed to Glenn in the clear near the corner. Glenn feinted a shot, changed his mind as a man leaped in front of him, and passed to Don. Glenn ran in front of Don toward the front of the basket. Again he was open.

Don leaped for a jump shot. He was twenty feet from the basket, more than ten feet farther than Glenn. He released the ball. But not at the basket! It shot in a swift, straight line directly at Glenn!

Though stunned with surprise, Glenn caught it. He sprang up, shot. The ball rif-fled through the net clean as a whistle.

He ran up the court as a player caught the ball and passed it to the ref. A hand slapped him on the shoulder.

"Nice going, Glenn," Frog said.

"Thanks, Frog."

The Jackrabbits brought the ball up to their front court, tried to work it close to the basket with short passes. The Sabers clung to their men like leeches. They tried hard to steal the ball, to force a bad pass. All at once a Jackrabbit took a jump shot. The ball struck the rim, bounced against the boards and down. Hungry hands flew up for the rebound. Don got it.

Glenn ran in front of him. Don passed him the ball and Glenn dribbled to the side. He saw Andy bolting down the middle of the court and heaved the ball to him.

The instant he released the ball he knew it was a lousy throw. The ball went sailing over Andy's head and into the empty bleachers behind the scorekeeper's table.

"No, Glenn!" Coach Munson shouted. "Watch those passes!" He sent in Chet Bruner and Benjy Myles, took out Glenn and Frog.

"Thought you learned to keep your passes low?" Coach Munson said. "You've been doing pretty good."

Glenn shrugged. He still needed a lot of practice in passing. That was the answer.

He thought of Don. Don had gotten over his grudge. He had passed to Glenn when he was able to. Maybe that challenging remark to Don had done a lot of good after all.

The half ended with the Jackrabbits leading, 33–27.

Paul didn't get in until there were two minutes left in the third quarter. Once Benjy passed him the ball and right away Paul was called for traveling. Later he blocked a pass, caught it on a bounce, and passed it to Chet. Chet dribbled the ball all the way to his front court, went up, and laid it in.

"The old go, Chet! Nice play, Paul!" the coach shouted. He looked at Glenn. "Well, guess your brother came through that time, didn't he?"

Glenn's eyes sparkled. "Guess he did," he said happily.

Paul went in for a while again in the fourth quarter. Glenn, in the game now, too, was surprised. He didn't think the coach would let Paul go in with the Sabers trailing by ten points, 58–48.

The ball was in the Sabers' possession. Don flipped a short pass to Glenn, and Glenn passed to Paul. Paul was only a few steps away. A Jackrabbit sprang in front of him and Paul moved back.

Shreeeeeek! went the whistle. The referee spun his hands. "Traveling!" he shouted.

In spite of Paul's violation, the Sabers got four points closer to the Jackrabbits' score. The game ended with the Jackrabbits winning, 64–58.

No one said a word to Paul as Glenn walked with him to the dressing room. Only Coach Munson, who put his hand on Paul's shoulder and smiled encouragingly. "Have to learn to pivot, Paul. And not to move that foot. They'll call traveling on you every time."

Paul smiled. "Guess I'll have to practice on it," he said.

If just one of the guys would say something to Paul while they were in the locker room, or taking their showers. But no one did. Except Benjy. He always did. The others just talked among themselves, ignoring Paul as if he weren't around.

Maybe Judy and I weren't so smart in having Paul learn basketball, Glenn thought as he unlaced his sneakers and slipped them off. Maybe Paul would be a lot happier if he just stayed home and constructed things out of the model set and played his keyboard.

On Thursday, December 30, the Sabers played the Blue Waves and won, 69–51. The next evening was New Year's Eve. Mom played Paul's keyboard and everyone stood around her and sang. It was snowing hard outside. Thick flakes of snow struck the picture window, melted, and streamed down the outer pane like fat tears.

The children wanted to stay up and watch the New Year come in. Mom and Dad said it was okay. But at eleven o'clock Paul was missing. Glenn found him on the bed, fully dressed and fast asleep.

"I figured he'd be too tired to stay up," Dad said, smiling.

He and Glenn started to get Paul undressed, but Paul awoke. He laughed at having fallen asleep, then finished undressing himself. He put on his pajamas and tucked himself in.

"Good night, son," Dad said.

"Good night, Dad," said Paul. "Good night, Glenn."

"Guess I'll hit the sack, too," said Glenn, stifling a yawn. He said good night to Dad, then went to the living room and said good night to Mom and Judy. Those were his last words to them this year. Then he went to bed.

New Year's Eve. What was so different about New Year's Eve?

It stopped snowing by morning. The sun was up, greeting the new year like a happy child. The snow on the sidewalk and street lay like a fuzzy white blanket.

"Boy, sure looks quiet out there," Glenn said to Paul. "Guess everybody's still asleep."

They swept off the driveway that afternoon and the three of them — Glenn, Paul, and Judy — played basketball. They practiced passing and foul shooting. Glenn figured that these were the important things for Paul to learn. At the same time he needed the practice himself.

They each took twenty-five shots at the basket. Glenn didn't bother to count how many he sank. But he counted Paul's. Paul's first two shots barely missed the rim. He sank the next four, missed the fifth, then sank the next and the next.

Glenn's mouth formed an oval. He looked at Judy and she looked at him. Her eyes danced.

"Guess who's getting to be an expert at foul shots," she said cheerily.

From that moment Glenn knew what he was going to have Paul practice on mostly. An expert? Why not?

They returned to school on Monday, January 3. Glenn hated to see the morning come, but once he was in school he didn't mind a bit. The students reviewed a little in each class, and the rest of the time talked about what they had done during their vacation. It seemed as if even the teachers weren't anxious to do schoolwork this first day.

The next evening the Sabers played the Gators, the team that was leading the loop. They had lost only one game so far, and that to the Blue Waves. News had gotten around that Dick Koles, their star center, was averaging nineteen points a game.

Dick started off hot as a torch. He sank two field goals and a foul shot to put the Gators in the lead, 5–0, in less than a minute of play. Frog sank a long one to start the Sabers off. It seemed as if that was what they needed. For the rest of the first quarter neither Dick nor the whole Gators team could keep more than two points ahead of the Sabers.

Glenn had gone in during the last few minutes of the quarter. He stayed in at the beginning of the second quarter, dropped in a basket to tie the score, then fouled his man on a layup shot. The Gator made both baskets, putting them ahead again by two points.

Then Glenn got fouled. The referee's hands went out, one finger extending from each. If Glenn made the first shot, he had another coming.

He missed the shot, and his hopes fell.

Paul went in for Benjy, but he never got the ball. No one passed it to him. Not once.

The Gators led at the half, 27–25. The Gators' big gun, Dick Koles, had scored nine points so far.

The Gators cut loose in the second half. Their little left forward, a red-headed kid whom Glenn was guarding, dumped in two long set shots. Then Dick Koles laid one against the boards for two points. A moment later he was fouled as he tried to do it again. His layup missed. He was given two shots, made them both.

I guess he is a star, Glenn muttered to himself.

The Sabers called time out. Coach Munson got into a huddle with them. Jim and Andy had to guard that Koles kid better, he said. And Glenn had better guard that little redhead closer, too.

"He flits around like a fly," Glenn said, smiling.

"You flit after him," the coach told him.

After time in was called, Glenn tried to flit after the redhead when the redhead flitted. It paid off. He intercepted a pass, bounced it to Jim. Jim dribbled it to the front court for a basket.

Jim and Andy kept glued to the Gators center. There were fewer passes to him. Little by little the strategy worked. Now and then the Sabers pumped one in, and gradually the score on the Sabers' side edged nearer the Gators'.

Two minutes after the fourth quarter started, Chet Bruner, in Glenn's place, sank a set shot from the key. The Sabers went ahead by one. With three minutes to go the coach sent in Paul.

"Oh, no!" Glenn heard Don moan. "What's he doing that for?"

Glenn was surprised, too. But if Paul was given the ball, and was fouled . . .

Paul was in the clear at the side of the keyhole. Jim had the ball, trying hard to keep away from two Gators who were after him like hornets. He flipped the ball to Paul.

"Shoot, Paul! Shoot!" Glenn yelled from the bench.

Paul looked at the basket for a fraction of a second, then shot. The ball rolled around the rim, dropped through!

The fans screamed. Glenn leaped up, clapping thunderously. "Thataway, Paul!" he cried. "Thataway, ol' kid!"

Later, with the ball in the Sabers' possession again, Paul was called on a holding violation. The Gators took it out. They passed wildly. It went out-of-bounds and it was the Sabers' ball again. They worked it up-court. Jim, surrounded by Gators beneath the basket, tried a hook shot. He made it!

The seconds ticked away. Fifteen to go . . . fourteen . . . thirteen . . . Amidst cheering shouts, the Sabers walked off with the game, 58–56.

"Paul Marlette," said the *Evening Journal* the next day, "was the spark that ignited the Sabers. His field goal in the last quarter was the turning point of the game. . . ."

The Sabers continued on a winning streak, defeating the Cowboys, the Shawnees, and the Jackrabbits. Some of the guys said it was Paul's basket in the Gators game that had brought them luck.

If it was luck, some of it had rubbed off on Paul. He sank a field goal in the game against the Cowboys and one in the Shawnees game. He was fouled in the Jackrabbits game and given one shot, but missed it.

He didn't play much, however. The coach didn't dare let him. Paul couldn't seem to learn to pivot on one foot, nor to pass without getting the ball intercepted, nor to guard his man without grabbing hold of him. To keep Paul in the game too long would be next to disastrous.

"He'd hurt the team," Coach Munson explained to Glenn during the last quarter of the Jackrabbits game. "He'd hurt himself, too. His mistakes would bother the devil out of him. But he's come a long way. Just playing a little while in each game has helped him. I can see that."

"He's best on foul shots," Glenn put in.

"I see he is. Goes to show you what steady training will do. How are the boys treating him on the outside?"

Glenn shrugged. "I guess they're better. Frog speaks to him all the time now. So does Stevie."

"What about Don?"

"He does when he feels like it."

"Don't worry. He'll come around, too. He's like Paul, in a way. Some things come to him very, very slowly. He has to work on it for a long time. He appreciates Paul. He just hates to admit it. One of these days he'll come out of it like a chick hatching out of an egg. You wait and see."

The final game of the season was against the Blue Waves, on Tuesday, January 18. It was the Big Game. Both teams were tied for second place, with nine wins and five losses each. The Gators had already clinched first place with thirteen wins and two losses. They had beaten the Cowboys in the first game that evening. The poor Cowboys finished in the cellar with only two wins and thirteen losses.

In the starting lineup were Andy Searles and Don Marshang at the forward positions,

Jim Tilton at center, Glenn and Stevie Keester at the guard positions. The bleachers were nearly filled.

Tom Snow, the Blue Waves' tall center, outjumped Jim and tipped the ball to a teammate. A couple of passes got the ball near the Blue Waves' basket. Glenn ran in to block the ball as a Blue Waves man started up with it and he struck the player's wrist. The whistle shrilled. He turned away in disgust, putting up his hand to show that he was the offender.

"Two shots," said the ref. At least the player had not made the basket.

The Blue Wave sank the first, missed the second. There was a scramble for the ball. Hands came up with it. The ball flew up against the boards, dropped through the net.

Glenn took the ball from out-of-bounds,

passed to Don, and the Sabers moved it up-court. The Blue Waves, wearing satiny blue uniforms with white trim, hovered around the basket. The Sabers couldn't move in.

Don took a set shot from the corner. It struck the rim, bounced high. Jim went in for the rebound, struggled for it with the Blue Waves' tall center. He got it, passed it back. Glenn caught it, dribbled in, and laid it up. A basket!

"Beautiful, Glenn!" shouted Paul from the bench.

The Blue Waves took out the ball, moved it to their front court. Glenn tried to keep between his man and the ball as much as possible. The Blue Wave was about his size, but was fast and shifty. Glenn had to keep on his toes every second.

Suddenly the man swung away from him. The ball came through the air like an orange bolt. Glenn leaped for it. It was just out of his reach. The Blue Wave caught it, went up. The ball arched over the ring. Jim and Tom Snow leaped and came down with it together, and the whistle shrilled for a jump ball.

A horn sounded and Frog went in. He pointed at Glenn and Glenn went out. "The next time you're in there try some corner shots," advised Coach Munson. "It's early, and those guys are guarding their basket like hawks."

Andy caught the tap. A moment later he was called for traveling and the ball went over to the Blue Waves. They moved the ball across the center line, then passed to a man at the sideline. Don was after it like a cat. He intercepted it and dribbled it back toward the Sabers' basket. He passed to Jim. Jim bounce-passed to Frog in the corner and Frog took a set. The ball arched gracefully and dropped through the net with a soft swish.

Before the quarter was over Benjy and Chet went in, replacing Andy and Stevie. Chet fouled a guy almost the first thing, resulting in another point for the Blue Waves. Then he sank a field goal. Benjy tried twice to drop one in, but couldn't. The Blue Waves led 16–15 as the horn sounded.

The coach let the same fellows who had finished the quarter play for about two minutes in the second quarter, then put Glenn and Stevie back in. Glenn wondered whether Paul would play. Maybe Coach Munson wouldn't let him because winning this game was very important. It would mean ten wins for the Sabers and second place. No matter how decent the coach seemed at times, he liked to be at the top of the heap — or next to it. It gave him something to tell his friends about during the summer.

The teams played evenly, neither one gaining three points more than the other. Then, with two minutes and ten seconds left in the first half, the Blue Waves lost the ball on a traveling charge. The buzzer sounded and Glenn looked to see who was coming in. Paul! His heart warmed.

Stevie went out. Glenn took the ball from out-of-bounds, passed to Paul.

"Make sure you don't travel!" cautioned Glenn as he ran past his brother.

Paul took a step forward, pivoted on his foot, passed to Don.

"Way to go, Paul!" Don shouted.

Was that a grin on his lips? Glenn smiled. Maybe Don was coming out of it already, he thought. Like the chick hatching from its egg.

Don dribbled up-court, passed to Jim. Jim

looked at the basket, feinted a shot to fake his guard out of the way, then bounced a pass to Glenn. Glenn ran in toward the basket, stopped as two men loomed in front of him. He passed to Don in the corner. Don took a set. In for two points!

The Blue Waves moved the ball in short, swift passes to their basket, tried a layup, missed. Jim caught the rebound. In no time the ball was back up near their basket. Don tried a corner shot, missed. Tom Snow caught the rebound, but someone knocked the ball from his hands. It rolled across the floor directly to Paul. Paul scooped it up, passed to Stevie. Glenn glanced at the clock. There were nineteen seconds left in the half, and the Blue Waves were leading, 33–30.

Quickly they moved the ball to their front court. Glenn passed to Jim and Jim shot to Don.

"Shoot! Shoot!" the cry rose from the Sabers fans.

Don was in the corner. He shot, just as the buzzer sounded. The ball struck the rim, spun around the inside of it, and went through.

Sabers — 32; Blue Waves — 33.

The seconds winked steadily away in the second half. First the Sabers dumped in a shot, and then the Blue Waves dumped one in. The quarter ended with the Blue Waves trailing by one point, 45–44.

They got hot in the fourth. For the first time in the game they put a spread of five points between them and the Sabers. Glenn, resting while Benjy relieved him, noticed Coach Munson banging his fists with a rapid tattoo against his leg. The coach was sweating as if he'd been running around on the floor, too.

All at once he stood and shouted, "Bring it down, Don! Bring it down!"

Don Marshang had just intercepted the ball, was dribbling it toward the Sabers basket. A Blue Wave ran alongside him, tried to steal the ball. Don stopped quickly, passed to Jim. Jim dribbled a bit, was blocked. He turned, whipped a pass to Don, and Don took a set. The ball sailed in beautifully.

The whole Sabers bench — including Coach Munson — yelled their throats dry.

Now the Sabers trailed by three points.

"Okay, Paul and Glenn," Coach Munson said. "Both of you go in. Send out Benjy and Frog. Paul, if you have a chance to shoot — shoot."

"I will," Paul promised.

The brothers reported to the scorekeeper and went in. Glenn slapped Paul lightly on the hip. "Let's get 'em, kid," he said.

The Blue Waves sank another. Jim then

drove in and sank a layup. He was fouled, but the ball went through the hoop and he was given one shot. He made it! Two points behind!

A minute to go. Don, flitting about like a mosquito, intercepted another pass. The Sabers moved the ball to their front court. They passed carefully. Glenn got the ball, saw Paul move to the corner, and passed it to him.

"Shoot, Paul!" cried Glenn.

Paul had caught the ball. He looked at the basket. He started to shoot, when a Blue Waves man sprang in front of him, struck the ball and his hands.

Shreeeeek! "Two shots!" shouted the ref.

Glenn's heart thundered as Paul went to the free-throw line. The Sabers fans were whooping like crazy. The referee pleaded for them to be quiet, then handed the ball to Paul.

Paul bounced it once, looked at the basket, and shot. Swish! Right through the net! For an instant the crowd yelled — then quieted again.

Paul took his second shot. Swish! The score was tied!

The Blue Waves took out the ball, lost it on a traveling violation. Once again, with caution, the Sabers moved the ball toward their basket. Then, from the corner, Don took a set. It went in!

Seconds later the buzzer sounded. The ball game was over. The Sabers won, 53–51.

The Sabers formed a belt around their happy coach. "Hooray, Coach! Hooray, Coach! Hooray, Coach!" they yelled.

Coach Munson was as thrilled as his charges. One by one he pumped their hands. When he came to Paul he shook Paul's hand harder than he did any of the others'.

"Paul, those two foul shots did it," he said. "You came through like a champion."

"Thanks, Coach." Paul's sweating face beamed like a beacon.

Then, to Glenn's happy surprise, Don came up to Paul and shook his hand, too. "You did great, Paul!" he said. "You really helped us win that ball game!"

Then all the other players shook Paul's hand. Glenn thought he had never seen Paul so happy.

That Saturday afternoon, Benjy came over. It was the first time he had been at the house since that day his mother had come after him.

"Can Paul come over to my house?" he asked. His eyes were big as walnuts as he looked from Glenn to Judy and then to Paul.

Mom appeared from the next room. "Hi, Benjy." She smiled.

"Hi, Mrs. Marlette."

"Can I go over to Benjy's house, Mom?" Paul asked hopefully. "Can I, Mom?"

"I guess you can," Mom said.

"Oh, boy!" cried Paul. He got dressed and hurried out with Benjy. Both looked as happy as ever as they ran down the porch steps and headed for Benjy's house.

"I wonder if Benjy's mother knows about it?" Glenn said.

"We'll find out soon enough," replied his sister.

A half hour went by. Then someone was at the door. It was Paul. He was smiling and breathing as if he were in a terrible rush about something.

"Well, he stayed for a while," said Glenn. "They were probably playing somewhere where she couldn't see them."

Paul went to his room, came out with

something in his hand, and left again. Glenn looked curiously at Judy. "That was the present he was going to give Benjy at Christmastime," he said. "He's kept it all this while!"

Noontime came and Paul had not returned for lunch.

"Maybe you should go over there, Glenn, and tell him to come home," Mom suggested. "Those two kids are probably stuck somewhere so that even Mrs. Myles doesn't know where they are."

Glenn put on his parka and walked over to the Myles's house. He didn't see the kids out front nor out back, and wondered what to do. If he knocked at the door and asked for Paul, Mrs. Myles might look at him as if he were insulting her or something.

Doggone Paul. Where did he and Benjy go?

He heard a creak and saw the back door of the Myles's house open. Mrs. Myles looked out. There was something on her face Glenn had never seen before — a real, genuine smile.

"Glenn, if you're looking for Paul," she said, "he's in the house, playing with Benjy. Benjy has a racing car set and they're having the time of their lives."

Glenn stared. "Oh? Well — he's got to come home and eat."

"He's going to eat with us," Mrs. Myles said. "I phoned your mother just a minute ago. She said it was all right. Would you like to come in, too? We have enough for all of us."

Glenn trembled. "No. No, thanks, Mrs. Myles. Mom's got the stuff almost on the table already. Then it's all right for Paul to stay?"

"Of course it is."

He smiled. "Okay. Thanks, Mrs. Myles. I'd better get home then. Good-bye!"

"Good-bye."

He raced home. The door clattered loudly behind him as he rushed into the house. "He's going to eat there!" he shouted. "He's playing with Benjy's racing cars and he's going to eat there!"

Mom's eyes twinkled. "That's what Mrs. Myles told me," she said.

"Well, it's about time!" cried Judy, and she started to dance about the room. "Guess it just takes some people longer to open up their eyes."

"And their hearts," added Mom.

Glenn went to the living room and plunked himself in front of the keyboard Mom and Dad had given Paul. He struck a chord. "Wow!" he cried, and grabbed hold of his nose.

"What a sour one that was!" Judy laughed. "Maybe you'd better have Paul teach you to play that thing!"

"You're right!" Glenn laughed, too. "Well, that's only fair, isn't it? I taught him basket-ball. He can teach me music!"

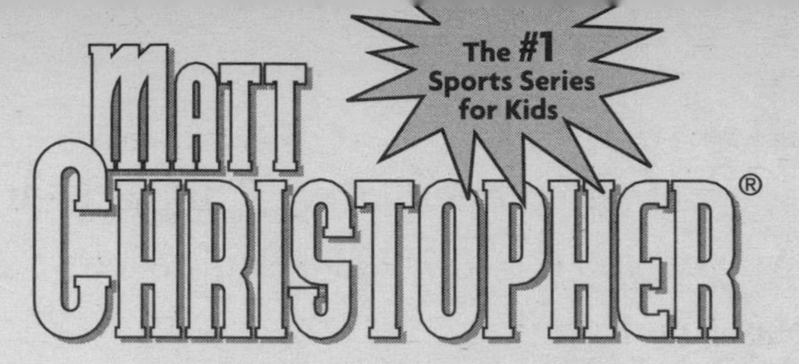

Read them all!

- Baseball Flyhawk
- Baseball Pals
- Baseball Turnaround
- The Basket Counts
- Body Check
- Catch That Pass!
- Catcher with a Glass Arm
- Center Court Sting
- Challenge at Second Base
- The Comeback Challenge
- Cool as Ice
- The Counterfeit Tackle
- The Diamond Champs
- Dirt Bike Racer
- Dirt Bike Runaway
- Dive Right In
- Double Play at Short
- Face-Off
- Fairway Phenom
- Football Fugitive
- Football Nightmare
- The Fox Steals Home
- Goalkeeper in Charge
- The Great Quarterback Switch
- Halfback Attack*
- The Hockey Machine
- Ice Magic
- Inline Skater
- Johnny Long Legs
- The Kid Who Only Hit Homers
- Long-Arm Quarterback
- Long Shot for Paul

*Originally published as *Crackerjack Halfback*

- Look Who's Playing First Base
- Miracle at the Plate
- Mountain Bike Mania
- No Arm in Left Field
- Nothin' but Net
- Olympic Dream
- Penalty Shot
- Pressure Play
- Prime-Time Pitcher
- Red-Hot Hightops
- The Reluctant Pitcher
- Return of the Home Run Kid
- Roller Hockey Radicals
- Run, Billy, Run
- Run for It
- Shoot for the Hoop
- Shortstop from Tokyo
- Skateboard Renegade
- Skateboard Tough
- Snowboard Maverick
- Snowboard Showdown
- Soccer Duel
- Soccer Halfback
- Soccer Scoop
- Spike It!
- The Submarine Pitch
- Supercharged Infield
- The Team That Couldn't Lose
- Tennis Ace
- Tight End
- Too Hot to Handle
- Top Wing
- Touchdown for Tommy
- Tough to Tackle
- Wheel Wizards
- Windmill Windup
- Wingman on Ice
- The Year Mom Won the Pennant

All available in paperback from Little, Brown and Company

Matt Christopher®

Sports Bio Bookshelf

Lance Armstrong

Kobe Bryant

Terrell Davis

Julie Foudy

Jeff Gordon

Wayne Gretzky

Ken Griffey Jr.

Mia Hamm

Tony Hawk

Grant Hill

Ichiro

Derek Jeter

Randy Johnson

Michael Jordan

Mario Lemieux

Tara Lipinski

Mark McGwire

Greg Maddux

Hakeem Olajuwon

Shaquille O'Neal

Alex Rodriguez

Briana Scurry

Sammy Sosa

Venus and Serena Williams

Tiger Woods

Steve Young